S0-AKU-164

From his home on the other side of the moon, Father Time summoned eight of his most trusted storytellers to bring a message of hope to all children. Their mission was to spread magical tales throughout the world: tales that remind us that we all belong to one family, one world; that our hearts speak the same language, no matter where we live or how different we look or sound; and that we each have the right to be loved, to be nurtured, and to reach for a dream.

This is one of their stories.
Listen with your heart and share the magic.

FOR SYLVIE AND
HER UNCLE RICK,
WHOSE CAPACITY
TO LOVE HAS
AWAKENED OUR
HEARTS.

Our thanks to artists Shanna Grotenhuis, Jane Portaluppi, and Mindi Sarko,
as well as Sharon Beckett, Yoshie Brady, Andrea Cascardi, Solveig Chandler, Jun Deguchi,
Akiko Eguchi, Liz Gordon, Tetsuo Ishida, William Levy, Michael Lynton, Masaru Nakamura,
Steve Ouimet, Tomoko Sato, Isamu Senda, Minoru Shibuya, Jan Smith, and Hideaki Suda.

THE MOON MAIDEN

Inspired by an Old Japanese Tale

Flavia Weedn & Lisa Weedn Gilbert

Illustrated by Flavia Weedn

Hyperion • New York

A long time ago, a farmer and his wife lived near the edge of a forest.

They were good people, loving and kind, but there was something missing in their lives. Their hearts felt incomplete because they had no children. More than anything else, they wished for a child to love.

As they were getting ready for bed one night, they saw a magical glow shining in the woods near their home.

The farmer and his wife followed the light and soon discovered a beautiful little girl, different from any other child they had ever seen, for she was dressed in moonlight and stardust.

The little moon maiden said, "Because you have wanted a child for such a long time, my mother, the moon lady, has sent me to live with you for a while to be your little girl."

With love they welcomed her, and soon the moon
maiden, the farmer, and his wife lived as a family.
They were all very happy together.

The farmer's wife baked for the moon maiden
and sewed for her, and together they would
play games and sing songs.

The farmer took her for rides on the back of his bicycle and told her about all the wonderful things in the world.

They planted seeds in the garden and watched the
flowers grow in the spring.

At night the farmer and his wife
would sit beside the moon maiden's
bed and read books or tell her stories
until she fell asleep.

The moon maiden became friends with the other children in the village. They taught her rhymes and songs, and she would sing them moon songs and tell them about the magic of the sky. At the marketplace she would help people carry their fruits and vegetables, and because of her kindness she was loved by everyone in the village.

Years passed. Then one day the moon maiden told the farmer and his wife that she had something important to tell them.

"For many years I have been happy here with you, but soon I must return to my other home in the sky and be with my mother, the moon lady."

The farmer and his wife had always known that the little moon maiden couldn't stay with them forever, but somehow it seemed that the time for her to leave came too soon. Because they loved her, knowing she had to go away made them very sad, and they begged her to stay.

But late that night, when the moon rose in the sky,
it sent a silver bridge of moonlight from the heavens
to the earth and down came the moon lady.

The little moon maiden was awakened by the
moonlight shining through her window. And when
she looked up and saw her mother, the moon lady,
she knew that the time had come for her to
leave the earth and go back to her
home in the sky.

She took her mother's hand, and together they
began to walk across the moonlight bridge. Because
she loved the farmer and his wife so very much, the
moon maiden took one last look back down to earth
and wept silvery tears.

She wondered if those she was
leaving behind would remember how
much she loved them and if they knew
that a part of her would be with them always.

Then a magical thing happened. Her tears took wing and floated down to earth, hovering low in the sky. They began to reflect the tiny lights from the silvery moon and suddenly the moon maiden's tears became beautiful fireflies.

The moon maiden knew, from that moment on, that each time the farmer and his wife would see fireflies surrounding their home, they would think of her and remember the wonderful times and all the love they had shared together.

She hoped that these beautiful fireflies would remind everyone everywhere how magical life is and how love, in spite of time or distance, lasts forever.

And that is why to this day a magical sense of wonder and love fills every heart who discovers the moon maiden's gift of fireflies.

Text © 1995 by Flavia Weedn and Lisa Weedn Gilbert.
Illustrations © 1995 by Flavia Weedn.
All rights reserved.
Produced in cooperation with Dream Maker Studios AG.
Printed in Singapore.
For information address Hyperion Books for Children,
114 Fifth Avenue, New York, New York 10011.

FIRST EDITION
1 3 5 7 9 10 8 6 4 2

Library of Congress Cataloging-in-Publication Data

Weedn, Flavia.
The moon maiden: inspired by an old Japanese tale/written by
Flavia Weedn & Lisa Weedn Gilbert; illustrated by Flavia Weedn.
p. cm.—(Dream maker stories)
Summary: In this retelling of a Japanese fairy tale, a childless couple
is allowed to take care of the Moon's daughter until it is time for
her to join her mother in the sky.
ISBN 0-7868-0045-3
[1. Fairy tales. 2. Folklore—Japan.] I. Gilbert, Lisa Weedn.
II. Title. III. Series: Weedn, Flavia. Dream maker stories
PZ8.W423Mo   1995
382.2'095206—dc20   94–15054   CIP AC

The artwork for each picture is digitally mastered using acrylic on canvas.
This book is set in 17-point Bernhard Modern.